David Chandler

D0241914

TO YE ROYAL BED-DOM

The Bedtime Book of 365 Nursery Rhymes

HAMLYN

London · New York · Sydney · Toronto

First published 1972
9th impression 1977
The Hamlyn Publishing Group Limited
London • New York • Sydney • Toronto
Astronaut House, Feltham, Middlesex, England
© Copyright 1972 The Hamlyn Publishing Group Limited
ISBN 0 600 31266 6
Printed in Czechoslovakia by Polygrafia, Prague
51 102/9

The Bedtime Book of 365 Nursery Rhymes

illustrated by

Ann Evans
Caroline Sharpe
Ann Anderson
Catherine Bradbury
Gay John Galsworthy

Esme Eve
Tancy Baran
Susan Lineham
Diane Mathes
Gerry Embleton

Tony Streek
Sarah Silcock
Joy Anderson
Douglas Hall
Jenny Reyn
Brenda Meredith Seymour

Whistle, daughter, whistle,
And you shall have a sheep.
Mother, I cannot whistle,
Neither can I sleep.

Whistle, daughter whistle,
And you shall have a cow.
Mother, I cannot whistle,
Neither know I how.

Whistle, daughter, whistle,
And you shall have a man.
Mother, I cannot whistle,
But I'll do the best I can.

A robin and a robin's son
Once went to town to buy a bun.
They couldn't decide on plum or plain,
And so they went back home again.

Little Tommy Tucker
Sings for his supper.
What shall he eat?
White bread and butter.
How will he cut it
Without e'er a knife?
How can he marry
Without e'er a wife?

A fox jumped up one winter's night,
And begged the moon to give him light,
For he'd many miles to trot that night
Before he reached his den O!
    Den O! Den O!
For he'd many miles to trot that night
Before he reached his den O!

The first place he came to was a farmer's yard,
Where the ducks and the geese declared it hard
That their nerves should be shaken
        and their rest so marred
By a visit from Mr Fox O!
        Fox O! Fox O!
That their nerves should be shaken
        and their rest so marred
By a visit from Mr Fox O!

He took the grey goose by the neck,
And swung him right across his back;
The grey goose cried out, "Quack, quack, quack,"
With his legs hanging dangling down O!
    Down O! Down O!
The grey goose cried out, "Quack, quack, quack,"
With his legs hanging dangling down O!

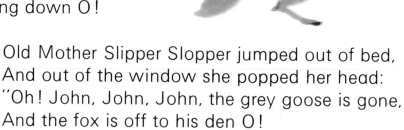

Old Mother Slipper Slopper jumped out of bed,
And out of the window she popped her head:
"Oh! John, John, John, the grey goose is gone,
And the fox is off to his den O!
    Den O! Den O!
Oh! John, John, John, the grey goose is gone,
And the fox is off to his den O!"

John ran up to the top of the hill,
And blew his whistle loud and shrill;
Said the fox, "That is very pretty music; still —
I'd rather be in my den O!
       Den O! Den O!"
Said the fox, "That is very pretty music; still —
I'd rather be in my Den O!"

The fox went back to his hungry den,
And his dear little foxes eight, nine, ten;
Quoth they, "Good daddy, you must go there again,
If you bring such good cheer from the farm O!
       Farm O! Farm O!"
Quoth they, "Good daddy, you must go there again,
If you bring such good cheer from the farm O!"

The fox and his wife, without any strife,
Said they never ate a better goose in all their life.
They did very well without fork or knife,
And the little ones picked the bones O!
       Bones O! Bones O!
They did very well without fork or knife,
And the little ones picked the bones O!

A jolly fat miller is Poopleton Bun,
With elephant legs that weigh half a ton,
And a face that is round and red as the sun.

Six little mice sat down to spin;
Pussy passed by and she peeped in.
What are you doing, my little men?
Weaving coats for gentlemen.
Shall I come in and cut off your threads?
No, no, Mistress Pussy, you'd bite off our heads.
Oh, no, I'll not; I'll help you to spin.
That may be so, but you don't come in!

Hoddley, poddley, puddle and fogs,
Cats are to marry the poodle dogs;
Cats in blue jackets and dogs in red hats,
What will become of the mice and rats?

What is the rhyme for porringer?
What is the rhyme for porringer?
The king he had a daughter fair,
And gave the Prince of Orange her!

13

Pit, pat, well-a-day,
Little Robin flew away;
Where can little Robin be?
Gone into the cherry tree.

Barney Bodkin broke his nose,
Without feet we can't have toes;
Crazy folks are always mad,
Want of money makes us sad.

14

Old Mother Goose,
When she wanted to wander,
Would ride through the air,
On a very fine gander.

If all the seas were one sea,
What a great sea that would be!
If all the trees were one tree,
What a great tree that would be!
If all the axes were one axe,
What a great axe that would be!
And if all the men were one man,
What a great man that would be!
And if the great man took the great axe
And cut down the great tree
And let it fall into the great sea,
What a splish splash that would be!

Flour of England, fruit of Spain,
Met together in a shower of rain;
Put in a bag tied round with a string;
If you tell me this riddle,
I'll give you a ring.

Wash the dishes, wipe the dishes,
Ring the bell for tea;
Three good wishes, three good kisses,
I will give to thee.

Jenny come tie my,
Jenny come tie my,
Jenny come tie my bonny cravat;
I've tied it behind,
I've tied it before,
I've tied it so often, I'll tie it no more.

Diddlety, diddlety, dumpty,
The cat ran up the plum tree;
Half a crown to fetch her down,
Diddlety, diddlety, dumpty.

My maid Mary, she minds the dairy,
While I go hoeing and mowing each morn;
Gaily run the reel and the little spinning wheel,
While I am singing and mowing my corn.

Chook, chook, chook, chook, chook,
Good morning, Mrs Hen.
How many chickens have you got?
Madam, I've got ten.
Four of them are yellow,
And four of them are brown,
And two of them are speckled red,
The nicest in the town.

Donkey, donkey, old and grey,
Open your mouth and gently bray;
Lift your ears and blow your horn,
To wake the world this sleepy morn.

"Bow-wow," says the dog,
"Mew, mew," says the cat,
"Grunt, grunt," goes the hog,
And, "Squeak" goes the rat.
"Tu-whu," says the owl,
"Caw, caw," says the crow,
"Quack, quack," says the duck,
And what cuckoos say you know.

Rain, rain, go away,
Come again another day;
Little Tommy wants to play.

St Swithin's day, if thou dost rain,
For forty days it will remain;
St Swithin's day, if thou be fair,
For forty days 'twill rain no more.

Rain on the green grass,
And rain on the tree,
Rain on the house-top,
But not on me.

Doctor Foster went to Gloucester
In a shower of rain;
He stepped in a puddle, up to his middle,
And never went there again.

21

Monday's child is fair of face,
Tuesday's child is full of grace,
Wednesday's child is full of woe,
Thursday's child has far to go,
Friday's child is loving and giving,
Saturday's child works hard for a living,
And the child that is born on the Sabbath day
Is bonny and blithe, and good and gay.

Cobbler, cobbler, mend my shoe,
Get it done by half past two;
Stitch it up, and stitch it down,
Then I'll give you half a crown.

22

There were three jovial huntsmen,
As I have heard them say,
And they would go a-hunting
Upon St David's Day.

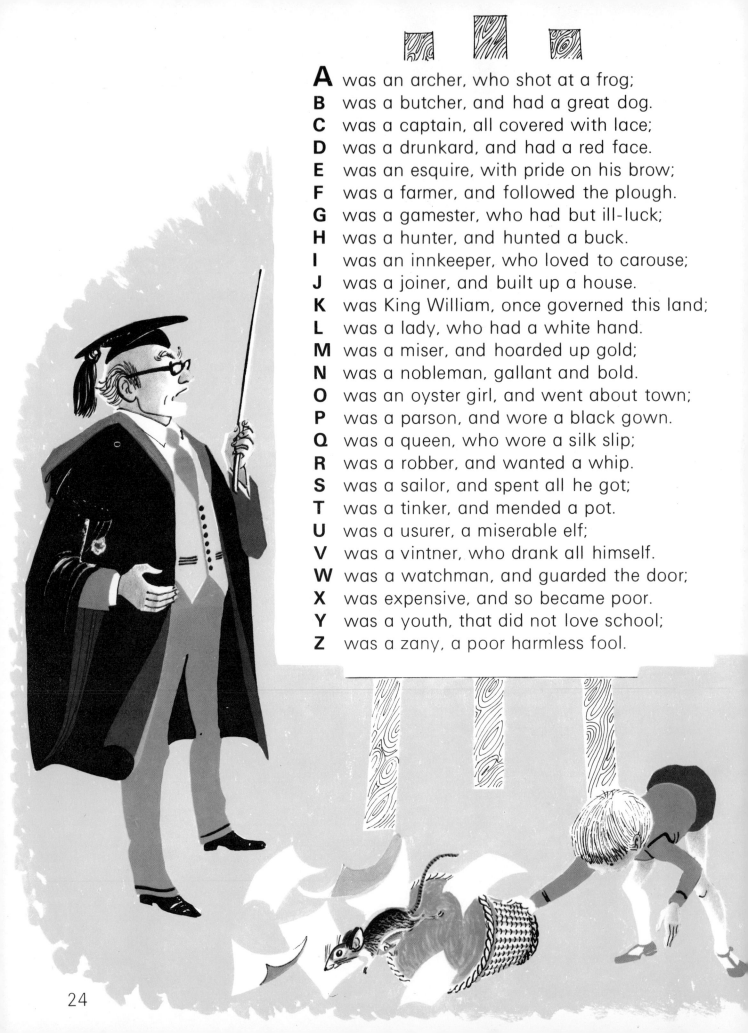

A   was an archer, who shot at a frog;
B   was a butcher, and had a great dog.
C   was a captain, all covered with lace;
D   was a drunkard, and had a red face.
E   was an esquire, with pride on his brow;
F   was a farmer, and followed the plough.
G   was a gamester, who had but ill-luck;
H   was a hunter, and hunted a buck.
I   was an innkeeper, who loved to carouse;
J   was a joiner, and built up a house.
K   was King William, once governed this land;
L   was a lady, who had a white hand.
M   was a miser, and hoarded up gold;
N   was a nobleman, gallant and bold.
O   was an oyster girl, and went about town;
P   was a parson, and wore a black gown.
Q   was a queen, who wore a silk slip;
R   was a robber, and wanted a whip.
S   was a sailor, and spent all he got;
T   was a tinker, and mended a pot.
U   was a usurer, a miserable elf;
V   was a vintner, who drank all himself.
W   was a watchman, and guarded the door;
X   was expensive, and so became poor.
Y   was a youth, that did not love school;
Z   was a zany, a poor harmless fool.

There's a neat little clock,
In the schoolroom it stands,
And it points to the time
With its two little hands.

And may we, like the clock,
Keep a face clean and bright,
With hands ever ready
To do what is right.

A diller, a dollar,
A ten o'clock scholar,
What makes you come so soon?
You used to come at ten o'clock,
But now you come at noon.

Multiplication is vexation,
Division is as bad;
The Rule of Three doth puzzle me,
And Practice drives me mad.

25

Little Poll Parrot
Sat in his garret,
Eating toast and tea;
A little brown mouse
Jumped into the house,
And stole it all away.

Queen, Queen Caroline,
Washed her hair in turpentine,
Turpentine made it shine,
Queen, Queen Caroline.

Wasn't it funny? Hear it, all people;
Little Tom Thumb has swallowed a steeple!
How did he do it? I'll tell you my son,
'Twas made of white sugar, and easily done!

Little King Pippin
He built a fine hall,
Pie-crust and pastry-crust
That was the wall;
The windows were made
Of black pudding and white,
And slated with pancakes,
You ne'er saw the like.

Star light, star bright,
First star I see tonight,
I wish I may, I wish I might,
Have the wish I wish tonight.

Goosey, goosey gander,
      Whither shall I wander?
Upstairs and downstairs
      And in my lady's chamber.
There I met an old man
      Who would not say his prayers,
I took him by the left leg
      And threw him down the stairs.

The man in the moon
Came down too soon,
And asked his way to Norwich;
He went by the south,
And burnt his mouth
With eating cold plum porridge.

It's raining, it's pouring,
The old man's snoring;
He got into bed
And bumped his head
And couldn't get up in the
morning.

Girls and boys, come out to play,
The moon doth shine as bright as day;
Leave your supper and leave your sleep,
And come with your playfellows into the street.
Come with a whoop, come with a call,
Come with a good will or not at all.
Up the ladder and down the wall,
A halfpenny roll will serve us all.
You find milk, and I'll find flour,
And we'll have a pudding in half an hour.

Georgie Porgie, pudding and pie,
Kissed the girls and made them cry;
When the boys came out to play,
Georgie Porgie ran away.

See-saw, Margery Daw,
Johnny shall have a new master;
He shall have but a penny a day,
Because he can't work any faster.

Ring-a-ring o' roses,
A pocket full of posies,
A-tishoo! A-tishoo!
We all fall down.

Here am I, little jumping Joan;
When nobody's with me,
I'm always alone.

Burnie bee, burnie bee,
Tell me when your wedding be?
If it be tomorrow day,
Take your wings and fly away.

For every evil under the sun
There is a remedy or there is none.
If there be one, seek till you find it;
If there be none, never mind it.

Here is the church, and here is the steeple;
Open the door and here are the people.
Here is the parson going upstairs,
And here he is a-saying his prayers.

Dearly beloved brethren, is it not a sin,
When you peel potatoes to throw away the skin?
For the skin feeds pigs and pigs feed you.
Dearly beloved brethren, is this not true?

When good King Arthur ruled this land,
He was a goodly king,
He bought three pecks of barley meal,
To make a bag pudding.

A bag pudding the king did make,
And stuffed it well with plums;
And in it put great lumps of fat,
As big as my two thumbs.

The king and queen did eat thereof,
And noblemen beside;
And what they could not eat that night,
The queen next morning fried.

Up and down the City Road,
In and out the Eagle,
That's the way the money goes,
Pop goes the weasel!

Half a pound of tuppenny rice,
Half a pound of treacle,
Mix it up and make it nice,
Pop goes the weasel!

34

The lion and the unicorn
Were fighting for the crown;
The lion beat the unicorn
All around the town.

Some gave them white bread,
And some gave them brown;
Some gave them plum cake
And drummed them out of town.

Thirty days hath September,
April, June and November;
All the rest have thirty-one,
Excepting February alone,
And that has twenty-eight days clear
And twenty-nine in each leap year.

Little Polly Flinders sat among the cinders,
Warming her pretty little toes;
Her mother came and caught her,
And whipped her little daughter,
For spoiling her nice new clothes.

The north wind doth blow,
And we shall have snow,
And what will the robin do then,
Poor thing?

He'll sit in the barn
And keep himself warm,
And hide his head under his wing,
Poor thing!

Oh do you know the muffin man,
The muffin man, the muffin man,
Oh do you know the muffin man,
Who lives in Drury Lane?

Oh yes, I know the muffin man,
The muffin man, the muffin man,
Oh yes, I know the muffin man,
Who lives in Drury Lane.

There was an old woman
And nothing she had,
And so this old woman
Was said to be mad.
She'd nothing to eat,
She'd nothing to wear,
She'd nothing to lose,
She'd nothing to fear,
She'd nothing to ask,
And nothing to give,
And when she did die
She'd nothing to leave.

Tweedle-dum and Tweedle-dee
Resolved to have a battle,
For Tweedle-dum said Tweedle-dee
Had spoiled his nice new rattle.

Hinks minx! the old witch winks,
The fat begins to fry;
There's nobody home but jumping Joan,
Father, Mother and I.

Just then flew by a monstrous crow,
As big as a tar-barrel,
Which frightened both the heroes so,
They quite forgot their quarrel.

39

Elsie Marley is grown so fine,
She won't get up to feed the swine,
But lies in bed till eight or nine,
Lazy Elsie Marley.

I had a little hen,
The prettiest ever seen;
She washed up the dishes,
And kept the house clean;
She went to the mill
To fetch some flour,
And always got home
In less than an hour;
She baked me my bread,
She brewed me my ale;
She sat by the fire
And told a fine tale.

When I work in the house I always say,
"How I'd like to toil out of doors all day!"
And when they send me to weed the flowers,
The day seems made of a hundred hours!

Mr Ibister, and Betsy his sister,
Resolved upon giving a treat;
So letters they write,
Their friends to invite,
To their house in Great Camomile Street.

Hark! Hark! The dogs do bark,
Beggars are coming to town;
Some in rags and some in tags,
And some in velvet gowns.

Gregory Griggs, Gregory Griggs,
Had twenty-seven different wigs.
He wore them up, he wore them down,
To please the people of the town;
He wore them east, he wore them west,
But he never could tell which he liked best.

Up street, down street,
Each window's made of glass;
If you'll go to Tommy's house,
You'll find a pretty lass.

Of all the sayings in this world
The one to see you through
Is, "Never trouble trouble
Till trouble troubles you".

One for sorrow,
Two for joy,
Three for a girl,
Four for a boy,
Five for silver,
Six for gold,
Seven for a secret ne'er to be told.

As I walked by myself
And talked to myself,
Myself said unto me,
"Look to thyself,
Take care of thyself,
For nobody cares for thee."

I answered myself
And said to myself,
In the selfsame repartee,
"Look to thyself
Or not to thyself,
The selfsame thing will be."

This little man lived all alone,
And he was a man of sorrow;
For if the weather was fair today,
He was sure it would rain tomorrow.

These nursery characters have all lost something. Little Bo-peep has lost her sheep, the boy has lost his dog and Little Betty Blue has lost her shoe. Turn the page around and see if you can find them.

Little Bo-peep has lost her sheep,
And can't tell where to find them;
Leave them alone, and they'll come home,
Bringing their tails behind them.

Little Bo-peep fell fast asleep,
And dreamt she heard them bleating;
But when she awoke, she found it a joke,
For they were still a-fleeting.

Then up she took her little crook,
Determined for to find them;
She found them indeed, but it made her heart bleed,
For they'd left their tails behind them.

It happened one day, as Bo-peep did stray
Over a meadow hard by,
That there she espied their tails, side by side,
All hung on a tree to dry.

She heaved a sigh, and gave by and by
Each careless sheep a banging;
And as for the rest, she thought it was best,
Just to leave the tails a-hanging.

Where, O where, has my little dog gone?
O where, O where, can he be?
With his tail cut short, and his ears cut long,
O where, O where, is he?

Little Betty Blue
Lost her holiday shoe;
What can little Betty do?
Give her another
To match the other
And then she may walk in two.

Three little ghostesses,
Sitting on postesses,
Eating buttered toastesses,
Greasing their fistesses,
Up to their wristesses.
Oh, what beastesses
To make such feastesses!

Four and twenty tailors went to kill a snail,
The best man amongst them durst not touch her tail;
She put out her horns like a little Kyloe cow,
Run, tailors, run, or she'll kill you all e'en now.

One, two,
Buckle my shoe;
Three, four,
Knock at the door;
Five, six,
Pick up sticks;
Seven, eight,
Lay them straight;
Nine, ten,
A big fat hen.

WANTED
GOOD
RAT
CATCHER
PLEASE
KNOCK!

Humpty Dumpty sat on a wall,
Humpty Dumpty had a great fall;
All the king's horses and all the king's men
Couldn't put Humpty together again.

Grey goose and grey gander,
Waft your wings together
And carry the good king's daughter
Over the one stand river.

Two grey kits and the grey kits' mother
All went over the bridge together.
The bridge broke down, they all fell in;
"May the rats go with you," says Tom Bolin.

51

Baa, baa, black sheep,
Have you any wool?
Yes, sir, yes, sir,
Three bags full;
One for my master,
One for my dame,
And one for the little boy
Who lives down the lane.

As I was going to Banbury,
Upon a summer's day,
My dame had butter, eggs and fruit,
And I had corn and hay.
Joe drove the ox, and Tom the swine,
Dick took the foal and mare;
I sold them all—then home to dine,
From famous Banbury fair.

Green cheese, yellow laces,
Up and down the market places,
Turn, cheeses, turn.

To market, to market, to buy a fat pig,
Home again, home again, jiggety-jig;
To market, to market, to buy a fat hog,
Home again, home again, juggety-jog.

Tom, Tom, the piper's son,
Stole a pig and away he run.
The pig was eat, and Tom was beat,
And Tom went crying down the street.

There was an old woman who had three cows,
     Rosy and Colin and Dun.
Rosy and Colin were sold at the fair,
And Dun broke her heart in a fit of despair,
So there was an end of her three cows,
     Rosy and Colin and Dun.

This is the house
that Jack built.

This is the malt
That lay in the house
that Jack built.

This is the rat
That ate the malt
That lay in the house
that Jack built.

This is the cat
That killed the rat
That ate the malt
That lay in the house
that Jack built.

This is the dog
That worried the cat
That killed the rat
That ate the malt
That lay in the house
    that Jack built.

This is the cow
    with the crumpled horn,
That tossed the dog
That worried the cat
That killed the rat
That ate the malt
That lay in the house
    that Jack built.

This is the maiden
    all forlorn,
That milked the cow
    with the crumpled horn,
That tossed the dog
That worried the cat
That killed the rat
That ate the malt
That lay in the house
    that Jack built.

55

This is the man
     all tattered and torn,
That kissed the maiden
     all forlorn,
That milked the cow
     with the crumpled horn,
That tossed the dog
That worried the cat
That killed the rat
That ate the malt
That lay in the house
     that Jack built.

This is the priest
     all shaven and shorn,
That married the man
     all tattered and torn,
That kissed the maiden
     all forlorn,
That milked the cow
     with the crumpled horn,
That tossed the dog
That worried the cat
That killed the rat
That ate the malt
That lay in the house
     that Jack built.

56

This is the cock
        that crowed in the morn,
That waked the priest
        all shaven and shorn,
That married the man
        all tattered and torn,
That kissed the maiden
        all forlorn,
That milked the cow
        with the crumpled horn,
That tossed the dog
That worried the cat
That killed the rat
That ate the malt
That lay in the house
        that Jack built.

This is the farmer
        sowing the corn,
That kept the cock
        that crowed in the morn,
That waked the priest
        all shaven and shorn,
That married the man
        all tattered and torn,
That kissed the maiden
        all forlorn,
That milked the cow
        with the crumpled horn,
That tossed the dog
That worried the cat
That killed the rat
That ate the malt
That lay in the house
        that Jack built.

Hey diddle dinkety, poppety, pet,
The merchants of London they wear scarlet;
Silk in the collar, and gold in the hem,
So merrily march the merchant men.

Who's that ringing at my door bell?
A little pussy cat that isn't very well.
Rub its little nose with a little mutton fat,
That's the best cure for a little pussy cat.

Hickety, pickety, my fine hen,
She lays eggs for gentlemen;
Gentlemen come every day
To see what my fine hen doth lay.
Sometimes nine and sometimes ten,
Hickety, pickety, my fine hen.

Old Mother Twitchett had but one eye
And a long tail which she let fly;
And every time she went through a gap,
A bit of her tail she left in a trap.

How many miles to Babylon?
Threescore miles and ten.
Can I get there by candlelight?
Yes, and back again.
If your heels are nimble and light,
You may get there by candlelight.

See a pin and pick it up,
All the day you'll have good luck.
See a pin and let it lay,
Bad luck you'll have all the day.

A wise old owl sat in an oak,
The more he heard the less he spoke;
The less he spoke the more he heard.
Why aren't we all like that wise old bird?

There was an old woman, as I've heard tell,
She went to market her eggs for to sell;
She went to market all on a market day,
And she fell asleep on the king's highway.

There came by a pedlar whose name was Stout;
He cut her petticoats all round about;
He cut her petticoats up to the knees,
Which made the old woman to shiver and sneeze.

When this little woman first did wake,
She began to shiver and she began to shake;
She began to wonder and she began to cry,
"Oh! deary, deary, me, this is none of I!

"But if it be I, as I do hope it be,
I've a little dog at home, and he'll know me;
If it be I, he'll wag his little tail,
And if it be not I, he'll loudly bark and wail."

Home went the little woman all in the dark;
Up got the little dog, and he began to bark;
He began to bark, so she began to cry,
"Lack-a-mercy on me, this is none of I!"

61

Oh, the grand old Duke of York,
He had ten thousand men;
He marched them up to the top of
    the hill,
And he marched them down again.
And when they were up, they were up,
And when they were down, they
        were down,
And when they were only half-way up,
They were neither up nor down.

I'm the king of the castle,
Get down you dirty rascal.

At the siege of Belle Isle
I was there all the while;
All the while,
All the while,
At the siege of Belle Isle.

John fought for his beloved land,
And when the war was over,
He kept a little biscuit stand
And lived and died in clover.

Father, may I go to war?
Yes, you may, my son;
Wear your woollen comforter,
But don't fire off your gun.

I won't be my father's Jack,
I won't be my mother's Jill,
I will find the fiddler's wife
And have music when I will.

Oh dear, what can the matter be?
Oh dear, what can the matter be?
Oh dear, what can the matter be?
Johnny's so long at the fair.

He promised he'd buy me a bunch of blue ribbons,
He promised he'd buy me a bunch of blue ribbons,
He promised he'd buy me a bunch of blue ribbons,
To tie up my bonny brown hair.

Little maid, pretty maid, whither goest thou?
Down in the meadow to milk my cow.
Shall I go with thee? No, not now;
When I send for thee, then come thou.

One he loves; two, he loves;
Three, he loves, they say.
Four, he loves with all his heart;
Five, he casts away.
Six, he loves; seven she loves;
Eight, they both love.
Nine, he comes; ten, he tarries;
Eleven, he courts; twelve, he marries.

Bell-horses, bell-horses,
What time of day?
One o'clock, two o'clock,
Off and away!

When I was a little boy,
I washed my mother's floor;
Now I am a man of wealth,
And drive a coach and four.

Little girl, little girl,
Where have you been?
I've been to see grandmother
Over the green.
What did she give you?
Milk in a can.
What did you say for it?
Thank you, Grandam.

Will you lend me your mare to ride
   but a mile?
No, she is lame leaping over a stile.
Alack! and I must go to the fair,
I'll give you good money for lending
   your mare.
Oh, ho! say you so?
Money will make the mare go.

I saw a ship a-sailing,
A-sailing on the sea,
And oh, it was all laden
With pretty things for thee!

There were comfits in the cabin,
And apples in the hold;
The sails were made of silk,
And the masts were all of gold.

68

The four-and-twenty sailors,
That stood between the decks,
Were four-and-twenty white mice
With chains about their necks.

The captain was a duck,
With a packet on his back,
And when the ship began to move
The captain said, "Quack! quack!"

Bobby Shaftoe's gone to sea,
Silver buckles at his knee;
He'll come back and marry me,
Bonny Bobby Shaftoe!

Bobby Shaftoe's bright and fair,
Combing down his yellow hair;
He's my love for evermore,
Bonny Bobby Shaftoe!

Little Tee Wee,
He went to sea
In an open boat;
And while afloat
The little boat bended,
And my story's ended.

Hickory, dickory, dock!
The mouse ran up the clock;
The clock struck one,
The mouse ran down,
Hickory, dickory, dock.

Eency, weency spider
Climbed the water spout;
Down came the rain
And washed poor spider out.
Out came the sunshine
And dried up the rain.
Eency, weency spider
Climbed up again.

Handy Spandy, Jack-a-dandy,
Loves plum cake and sugar candy.
He bought some at the grocer's shop
And out he came, hop, hop, hop.

A duck and a drake,
And a nice barley cake,
With a penny to pay the old baker.

A hop and a scotch
In another notch,
Slitherum, slatherum, take her.

I saw three ships come sailing by,
Come sailing by, come sailing by,
I saw three ships come sailing by,
On New Year's Day in the morning.

Poor old Robinson Crusoe!
Poor old Robinson Crusoe!
They made him a coat
Of an old nanny-goat.
I wonder why they should do so!
With a ring-a-ting-tang,
And a ring-a-tang-ting,
Poor old Robinson Crusoe!

Dance to your daddy,
My bonny laddie,
Dance to your daddy,
My bonny lamb.

And what do you think was in them then,
Was in them then, was in them then?
And what do you think was in them then,
On New Year's Day in the morning?

Three pretty girls were in them then,
Were in them then, were in them then,
Three pretty girls were in them then,
On New Year's Day in the morning.

And one could whistle, and one could sing,
And one could play on the violin;
Such joy there was at my wedding,
On New Year's Day in the morning.

You shall have a fishy
In a little dishy,
You shall have a fishy
When the boat comes in.

Three wise men of Gotham
Went to sea in a bowl;
If the bowl had been stronger,
My story would have been longer.

As round as an apple,
As deep as a cup,
And all the king's horses
Cannot pull it up.

Mary had a pretty bird,
Feathers bright and yellow,
Slender legs, upon my word,
He was a pretty fellow.

The sweetest notes he always sang,
Which much delighted Mary;
And near the cage she'd ever sit,
To hear her own canary.

Roses are red,
Violets are blue,
Sugar is sweet
And so are you.

As Tommy Snooks and Bessy Brooks
Were walking out one Sunday.
Says Tommy Snooks to Bessy Brooks,
"Tomorrow will be Monday."

Every lady in this land
Has twenty nails; upon each hand
Five, and twenty on hands and feet:
All this is true, without deceit.

Little Miss Muffet
Sat on a tuffet,
Eating her curds and whey;
There came a big spider,
Who sat down beside her,
And frightened Miss Muffet away.

One misty, moisty morning,
When cloudy was the weather,
I chanced to meet an old man
Clothed all in leather.
He began to compliment
And I began to grin.
How do you do, and how do you do,
And how do you do again?

The herring loves the merry moonlight,
The mackerel loves the wind;
But the oyster loves the dredging song,
For she comes of a gentle kind.

Brenda Meredith Seymour.

A farmer went trotting upon his grey mare,
Bumpety, bumpety, bump!
With his daughter behind him so rosy and fair,
Lumpety, lumpety, lump!

A raven cried "Croak!" and they all tumbled down,
Bumpety, bumpety, bump!
The mare broke her knees and the farmer his crown,
Lumpety, lumpety, lump!

The mischievous raven flew laughing away.
Bumpety, bumpety, bump!
And vowed he would serve them the same the next day,
Lumpety, lumpety, lump!

78

As I went to Bonner,
I met a pig
Without a wig,
Upon my word and honour.

This little pig went to market,
This little pig stayed at home,
This little pig had roast beef,
This little pig had none,
And this little pig cried, "Wee-wee-
    wee-wee-wee,
I can't find my way home."

Birds of a feather flock together,
And so will pigs and swine;
Rats and mice will have their choice,
And so will I have mine.

I saw a fishpond all on fire
I saw a house bow to a squire
I saw a parson twelve feet high
I saw a cottage near the sky
I saw a balloon made of lead
I saw a coffin drop down dead
I saw two sparrows run a race
I saw two horses making lace
I saw a girl just like a cat
I saw a kitten wear a hat
I saw a man who saw these too,
And said though strange they all were true.

Sally, Sally Waters,
Sprinkle in the pan,
Rise Sally, rise Sally,
Choose a young man.
Bow to the east,
Bow to the west,
Bow to the young man
That you love best.

Brenda Meredith Seymour

Kitty the spinner
Will sit down to dinner,
And eat the leg of a frog.

All good people,
Look over the steeple,
And see the cat play with the dog.

Who killed Cock Robin?
"I," said the sparrow,
"With my bow and arrow,
I killed Cock Robin."

Who saw him die?
"I," said the fly,
"With my little eye,
I saw him die."

Who caught his blood?
"I," said the fish,
"With my little dish,
I caught his blood."

Who made his shroud?
"I," said the beetle,
"With my thread and needle,
I made his shroud."

Who'll be the clerk?
"I,"said the lark,
"If it's not in the dark,
I'll be the clerk."

Who'll dig his grave?
"I," said the owl,
"With my spade and trowel,
I'll dig his grave."

Who'll be the parson?
"I," said the rook,
"With my little book,
I'll be the parson."

Who'll sing a psalm?
"I," said the thrush,
"As I sit in a bush,
I'll sing a psalm."

Who'll be chief mourner?
"I," said the dove,
"I mourn for my love,
I'll be chief mourner."

Who'll toll the bell?
"I," said the bull,
"Because I can pull,
I'll toll the bell."

All the birds of the air
Fell sighing and sobbing,
When they heard the bell toll
For poor Cock Robin.

To all it concerns,
This notice apprises,
The sparrow's for trial
At next bird assizes.

Little fishes in a brook,
Father caught them on a hook,
Mother fried them in a pan,
Johnny eats them like a man.

Willy boy, Willy boy, where are you going?
I will go with you, if that I may.
I am going to the meadow to see them a-mowing,
I am going to help them to turn the new hay.

Old Farmer Giles,
He went seven miles
With his faithful dog, Old Rover;
And Old Farmer Giles,
When he came to the stiles,
Took a run, and jumped clean over.

The little black dog ran round the house,
And set the bull a-roaring,
And drove the monkey in the boat,
Who set the oars a-rowing,
And scared the cock upon the rock,
Who cracked his throat with crowing.

Pussy cat, pussy cat, where have you been?
I've been to London to look at the queen.
Pussy cat, pussy cat, what did you there?
I frightened a little mouse under her chair.

Old King Cole
Was a merry old soul,
And a merry old soul was he;
He called for his pipe,
And he called for his bowl,
And he called for his fiddlers three.

Every fiddler, he had a fiddle,
And a very fine fiddle had he;
Oh, there's none so rare
As can compare
With King Cole and his fiddlers three.

Hector Protector was dressed all in green;
Hector Protector was sent to the queen.
The queen did not like him,
No more did the king;
So Hector Protector was sent back again.

Twelve pairs hanging high,
Twelve knights riding by;
Each knight took a pear
And yet left a dozen there.

87

Peter Piper picked a peck of pickled pepper;
A peck of pickled pepper Peter Piper picked.
If Peter Piper picked a peck of pickled pepper,
Where's the peck of pickled pepper Peter Piper picked?

Molly, my sister, and I fell out,
And what do you think it was all about?
She loved coffee and I loved tea.
And that was the reason we couldn't agree.

I had a little moppet,
I put it in my pocket,
And fed it with corn and hay.
There came a proud beggar,
And swore he would have her,
And stole little moppet away.

Don't Care didn't care,
Don't Care was wild:
Don't Care stole plum and pear
Like any beggar's child.

Don't Care was made to care,
Don't Care was hung:
Don't Care was put in a pot
And boiled till he was done.

Oranges and lemons,
Say the bells of St Clement's.

You owe me five farthings,
Say the bells of St Martin's.

When will you pay me?
Say the bells of Old Bailey.

When I grow rich,
Say the bells at Shoreditch.

Pray, when will that be?
Say the bells at Stepney.

I'm sure I don't know,
Says the great bell at Bow.

Here comes a candle
to light you to bed,

Here comes a chopper
to chop off your head!

See saw, sacradown,
Which is the way to London Town?
One foot up and the other foot down,
That is the way to London Town.

London Bridge is falling down,
Falling down, falling down.
London Bridge is falling down,
My fair lady.

Build it up with wood and clay,
Wood and clay, wood and clay,
Build it up with wood and clay,
My fair lady.

Up at Piccadilly, oh!
The coachman takes his stand,
And when he meets a pretty girl
He takes her by the hand;
Whip away forever, oh!
Drive away so clever, oh!
All the way to Bristol, oh!
He drives her four-in-hand.

As I was going to St Ives,
I met a man with seven wives.
Each wife had seven sacks,
Each sack had seven cats,
Each cat had seven kits;
Kits, cats, sacks and wives,
How many were going to St Ives?

"I know I have lost my train,"
Said a man named Joshua Lane;
"But I'll run on the rails
With my coat-tails for sails,
And maybe I'll catch it again."

See, see! What shall I see?
A horse's head where his tail should be.

Lucy Locket lost her pocket,
Kitty Fisher found it;
There was not a penny in it,
But a ribbon round it.

93

As I went down to Derby town,
Twas on a market day,
And there I met the finest ram
That was ever fed on hay.

The wool upon this ram's back,
It grew up to the sky;
The eagles built their nests in it,
I heard the young ones cry.

The horns upon this ram's head,
They grew up to the moon.
A man climbed up in April
And never came down till June.

This ram he had four mighty feet
And on them he did stand,
And every foot that he had got
Did cover an acre of land.

And if you don't believe me
And think it is a lie,
Then you go down to Derby town
And see as well as I.

There was an old woman
Lived under a hill;
And if she's not gone,
She lives there still.

Jerry Hall,
He was so small,
A rat could eat him,
Hat and all.

Three blind mice. Three blind mice.
See how they run! See how they run!
They all run after the farmer's wife,
Who cut off their tails with a carving knife.
Did you ever see such a thing in your life,
As three blind mice?

I would, if I could,
If I couldn't, how could I?
I couldn't, without I could, could I?
Could you, without you could, could ye?
        Could ye? Could ye?
Could you, without you could, could ye?

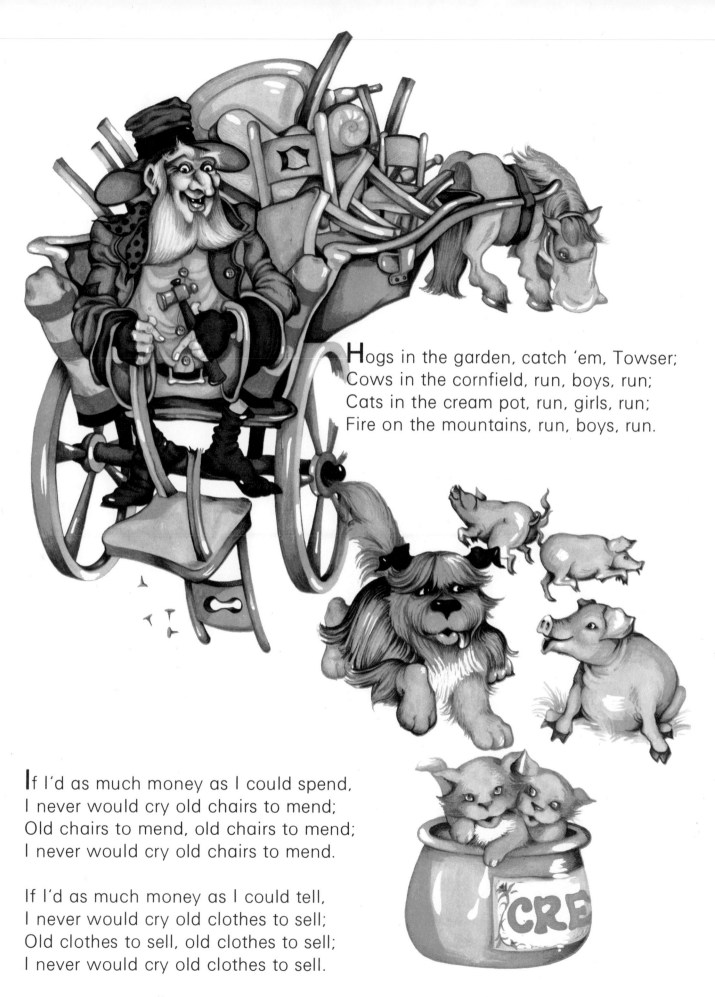

Hogs in the garden, catch 'em, Towser;
Cows in the cornfield, run, boys, run;
Cats in the cream pot, run, girls, run;
Fire on the mountains, run, boys, run.

If I'd as much money as I could spend,
I never would cry old chairs to mend;
Old chairs to mend, old chairs to mend;
I never would cry old chairs to mend.

If I'd as much money as I could tell,
I never would cry old clothes to sell;
Old clothes to sell, old clothes to sell;
I never would cry old clothes to sell.

Purple, yellow, red and green,
The king cannot reach it, nor yet the queen;
Nor can Old Noll, whose power's so great;
Tell me this riddle while I count eight.

Curly locks, Curly locks,
Wilt thou be mine?
Thou shalt not wash dishes
Nor yet feed the swine,
But sit on a cushion
And sew a fine seam
And feed upon strawberries,
Sugar and cream.

I love little pussy, her coat is so warm,
And if I don't hurt her, she'll do me no harm.
So I'll not pull her tail, nor drive her away,
But pussy and I very gently will play.
She shall sit by my side and I'll give her some food,
And pussy will love me because I am good.

Whoop! little Jerry Tigg
Has got a guinea pig;
I wonder where he bought it!
And Jerry Tigg has taught it
To wear a purple wig,
And dance an Irish jig.

Old Mother Hubbard
Went to the cupboard
To fetch her poor dog a bone;
But when she got there
The cupboard was bare,
And so the poor dog had none.

She went to the fruiterer's
To buy him some fruit;
But when she came back
He was playing the flute.

She went to the hatter's
To buy him a hat;
But when she came back
He was feeding the cat.

She went to the tailor's
To buy him a coat;
But when she came back
He was riding a goat.

100

The dame made a curtsy,
The dog made a bow;
The dame said, "Your servant,"
The dog said, "Bow-wow."

I bought a dozen new-laid eggs,
Off good old Farmer Dickens;
I hobbled home upon two legs,
And found them full of chickens.

101

Tommy Trot, a man of law,
Sold his bed and lay on straw;
Sold the straw and slept on grass,
To buy his wife a looking-glass.

A little girl quite well and hearty
Thought she'd like to give a party.
But as her friends were shy and wary,
Nobody came but her own canary.

Dame Trot and her cat
Sat down for a chat;
The Dame sat on this side
And puss sat on that.

"Puss," says the Dame,
"Can you catch a rat,
Or a mouse in the dark?"
"Purr," says the cat.

There was a fat man of Bombay,
Who was smoking one sunshiny day;
When a bird called a snipe
Flew away with his pipe,
Which vexed the fat man of Bombay.

I do not like thee, Doctor Fell,
The reason why I cannot tell;
But this I know, and know full well,
I do not like thee, Doctor Fell.

From here to there
To Washington Square;
When I get there
I'll pull your hair.

When I was a little boy I lived by myself,
And all the bread and cheese I got I laid upon the shelf;
The rats and the mice, they made such a strife,
I had to go to London to get myself a wife.

The streets were so broad and the lanes were so narrow,
I was forced to bring my wife home in a wheelbarrow,
The wheelbarrow broke and my wife had a fall;
Farewell, wheelbarrow, little wife and all.

"What's in the cupboard?"
Says Mr Hubbard.
"A knuckle of veal,"
Says Mr Beal.
"Is that all?"
Says Mr Ball.
"And enough too,"
Says Mr Glue;
And away they all flew.

Hannah Bantry, in the pantry,
Gnawing at a mutton bone;
How she gnawed it,
How she clawed it,
When she found herself alone.

Alas! alas! for Miss Mackay!
Her knives and forks have run away;
And when the cups and spoons are going,
She's sure there is no way of knowing.

106

Little Dame Crump
With her little hair-broom
Was carefully sweeping
Her little bedroom.
"Hobs-bobs," cried the Dame,
"A penny I spy.
To market I'll go
And a pig I'll buy."

The cat sat asleep by the side of the fire,
The mistress snored loud as a pig;
Jack took up his fiddle by Jenny's desire,
And struck up a bit of a jig.

Jack Sprat could eat no fat,
His wife could eat no lean,
And so between them both, you see,
They licked the platter clean.

Jack Sprat
Had a cat,
It had but one ear;
It went to buy butter
When butter was dear.

Nellie Bligh caught a fly
Going home from school.
Put it in a hot mince pie,
Waiting by to cool.

108

Pat-a-cake, pat-a-cake, baker's man,
Bake me a cake as fast as you can;
Roll it and pat it and mark it with "B",
And put it in the oven for Baby and me.

Baby and I
Were baked in a pie;
The gravy was wonderful hot;
We had nothing to pay
To the baker that day
And so we crept out of the pot.

Sing a song of sixpence,
A pocket full of rye;
Four and twenty blackbirds
Baked in a pie.

When the pie was opened,
The birds began to sing;
Wasn't that a dainty dish
To set before the king?

The king was in his counting-house,
Counting out his money;
The queen was in the parlour,
Eating bread and honey.

The maid was in the garden,
Hanging out the clothes;
When down came a blackbird,
And pecked off her nose!

One, two, three, four,
Mary at the cottage door,
Five, six, seven, eight,
Eating cherries off a plate.

Polly, put the kettle on,
Polly, put the kettle on,
Polly, put the kettle on,
We'll all have tea.

Sukey, take it off again,
Sukey, take it off again,
Sukey, take it off again,
They've all gone away.

Jeremiah, blow the fire,
Puff, puff, puff!
First you blow it gently,
Then you blow it rough.

There were once two cats of Kilkenny,
Each thought there was one cat too many;
So they fought and they fit,
And they scratched and they bit,
Till, excepting their nails
And the tips of their tails,
Instead of two cats, there weren't any.

Hob, shoe, hob;
Hob, shoe, hob;
Here a nail, and there a nail,
And that's well shod.

Red sky at night,
Shepherd's delight;
Red sky in the morning,
Shepherd's warning.

Twinkle, twinkle, little star,
How I wonder what you are!
Up above the world so high,
Like a diamond in the sky.

For the want of a nail, the shoe was lost;
For want of the shoe, the horse was lost;
For want of the horse, the rider was lost;
For want of a rider, the battle was lost;
For want of the battle, the kingdom was lost,
And all for the want of a horseshoe nail.

113

January brings the snow,
Makes our feet and fingers glow.

February brings the rain,
Thaws the frozen lake again.

March brings breezes loud and shrill,
Stirs the dancing daffodil.

April brings the primrose sweet,
Scatters daisies at our feet.

Spring is showery, flowery, bowery;
Summer is hoppy, croppy, poppy;
Autumn is wheezy, sneezy, freezy;
Winter is slippy, drippy, nippy.

As the days grow longer
The storms grow stronger.

May brings flocks of pretty lambs,
Skipping by their fleecy dams.

June brings tulips, lilies, roses,
Fills the children's hands with posies.

Hot July brings cooling showers,
Apricots and gillyflowers.

August brings the sheaves of corn,
Then the harvest home is borne.

Warm September brings the fruit,
Sportsmen then begin to shoot.

Fresh October brings the pheasant,
Then to gather nuts is pleasant.

Dull November brings the blast,
Then the leaves are whirling fast.

Chill December brings the sleet,
Blazing fire and Christmas treat.

Mister East gave a feast;
Mister North laid the cloth;
Mister West did his best;
Mister South burnt his mouth
Eating cold potato.

Bat, bat, come under my hat,
And I'll give you a slice of bacon;
And when I bake, I'll give you a cake,
If I am not mistaken.

Higher than a house,
Higher than a tree;
Oh, whatever can that be?

I went to Noke
But nobody spoke;
I went to Thame,
It was just the same;
Burford and Brill
Were silent and still,
But I went to Beckley
And they spoke directly.

I had a little nut tree; nothing would it bear
But a silver nutmeg and a golden pear.
The King of Spain's daughter came to visit me,
And all was because of my little nut tree.
I skipped over water, I danced over sea,
And all the birds in the air couldn't catch me.

If all the world were paper,
And all the sea were ink,
If all the trees were bread and cheese,
What should we have to drink?

Rub-a-dub-dub,
Three men in a tub;
And who do you think they be?
The butcher, the baker,
The candlestick-maker;
They all jumped out of a rotten potato,
'Twas enough to make a man stare.

There was a man and he had naught,
And robbers came to rob him;
He crept up to the chimney pot,
And then they thought they had him.

But he got down on t'other side,
And then they could not find him;
He ran fourteen miles in fifteen days,
And never looked behind him.

There was an old woman
Tossed up in a basket,
Seventeen times as high as the moon;
And where she was going,
I couldn't but ask it,
For in her hand she carried a broom.

"Old woman, old woman, old woman," said I,
"O whither, O whither, O whither so high?"
"To sweep the cobwebs off the sky!
And I'll be with you by and by."

At Brill on the hill
The wind blows shrill,
The cook no meat can dress;
At Stow-on-the Wold
The wind blows cold,
I know no more than this.

Round and round the rugged rock
The ragged rascal ran,
How many *R*'s are there in *that*?
Now tell me if you can.

I had a little castle upon the sea sand,
One half was water, the other was land;
I opened my little castle door,
and guess what I found;
I found a fair lady with a cup in her hand.
The cup was golden, filled with wine;
Drink, fair lady, and thou shalt be mine!

Terence McDiddler,
The three-stringed fiddler,
Can charm, if he please,
The fish from the seas.

Mother, may I go out to swim?
Yes, my darling daughter.
Fold your clothes up neat and trim,
But don't go near the water.

The greedy man is he who sits
And bites bits out of plates,
Or else takes up an almanac
And gobbles all the dates.

There was an old woman called Nothing-at-All,
Who lived in a dwelling exceedingly small;
A man stretched his mouth to its utmost extent,
And down at one gulp house and old woman went.

Solomon Grundy,
Born on Monday,
Christened on Tuesday,
Married on Wednesday,
Took ill on Thursday,
Worse on Friday,
Died on Saturday,
Buried on Sunday.
This is the end
Of Solomon Grundy.

SOLOMON
GRUNDY
MONDAY TO
SUNDAY

Simple Simon met a pieman,
Going to the fair;
Says Simple Simon to the pieman,
"Let me taste your ware."

Says the pieman to Simple Simon,
"Show me first your penny."
Says Simple Simon to the pieman,
"Indeed, I have not any."

Gee up, Neddy, to the fair;
What shall we buy when we get there?
A penny apple and a penny pear;
Gee up, Neddy, to the fair.

Smiling girls, rosy boys,
Come and buy my little toys;
Monkeys made of gingerbread,
And sugar horses painted red.

126

Punch and Judy
Fought for a pie;
Punch gave Judy
A knock in the eye.
Says Punch to Judy,
"Will you have any more?"
Says Judy to Punch,
"My eye is too sore."

This is the way the ladies ride,
Tri, tre, tri, tree, tri, tre, tri, tree.
This is the way the ladies ride,
Tri, tre, tri, tree, tri, tre, tri, tree.

This is the way the gentlemen ride;
Gallop-a-trot. Gallop-a-trot.
This is the way the gentlemen ride;
Gallop-a-trot. Gallop-a-trot.

This is the way the farmers ride,
Hobbledy-hoy, hobbledy-hoy.
This is they way the farmers ride,
Hobbledy-hoy, hobbledy-hoy.

127

Cocks crow in the morn to tell us to rise,
And he who lies late will never be wise.
For early to bed and early to rise
Makes a man healthy, wealthy and wise.

Little Blue Ben, who lives in the glen,
Keeps a blue cat and one blue hen,
Which lays of blue eggs a score and ten;
Where shall I find the little Blue Ben?

Tally-ho! Tally-ho!
A-hunting we will go,
We'll catch a fox
And put him in a box,
And then we'll let him go.

I had a little hobby-horse,
And it was dapple grey,
Its head was made of pea-straw,
Its tail was made of hay.

I sold it to an old woman
For a copper groat;
And I'll not sing my song again
Without another coat.

Round about the rosebush,
Three steps,
Four steps,
All the little boys and girls
Are sitting on the doorsteps.

Daffy-down-dilly has come up to town
In a yellow petticoat and a green gown.

There was an old woman who lived in Dundee,
And in her back garden there grew a plum tree;
The plums they grew rotten before they grew ripe,
And she sold them for three farthings a pint.

One, two, three, four, five,
Once I caught a fish alive.
Six, seven, eight, nine, ten,
Then I let it go again.
Why did you let it go?
Because it bit my finger so.
Which finger did it bite?
The little finger on the right.

There was a jolly miller once,
Lived on the river Dee;
He worked and sang from morn till night,
No lark more blithe than he.

And this the burden of his song,
Forever used to be,
"I care for nobody, no! not I,
If nobody cares for me."

Little Dicky Dilver
Had a wife of silver;
He took a stick and broke her back
And sold her to the miller;
The miller wouldn't have her
So he threw her in the river.

Row, row, row your boat,
Gently down the stream,
Merrily, merrily, merrily, merrily,
Life is but a dream.

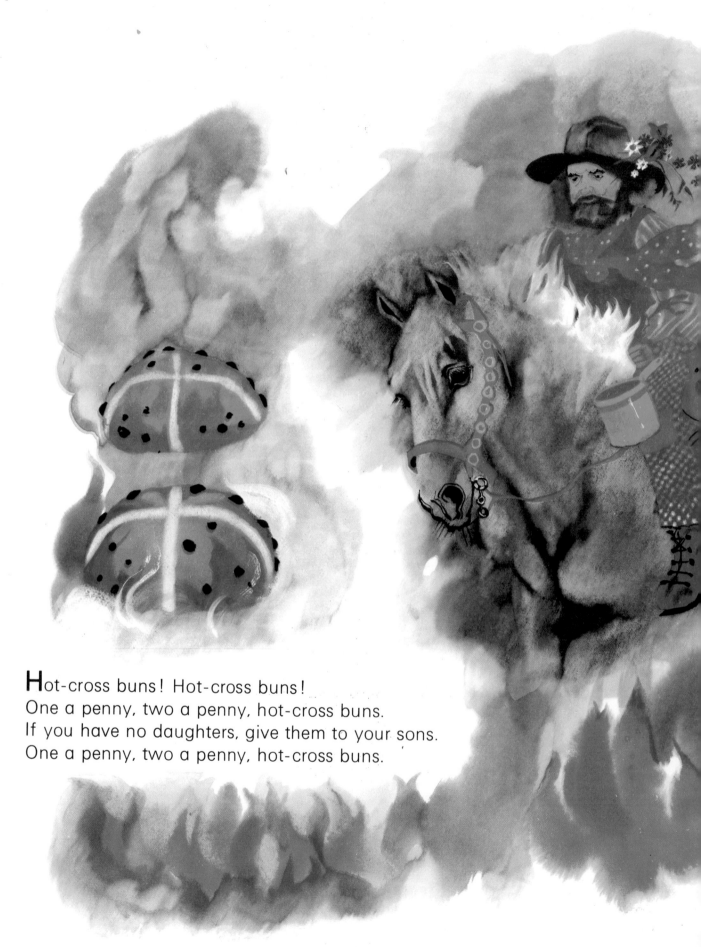

Hot-cross buns! Hot-cross buns!
One a penny, two a penny, hot-cross buns.
If you have no daughters, give them to your sons.
One a penny, two a penny, hot-cross buns.

Pussy cat Mole jumped over a coal
And in her best petticoat burnt a
    great hole.
Poor pussy's weeping, she'll have
    no more milk
Until her best petticoat's mended
    with silk.

If wishes were horses,
    Beggars would ride;
If turnips were watches,
    I'd wear one by my side.

If "ifs" and "ands"
    Were pots and pans
There'd be no need for tinkers' hands.

Cross Patch,
Draw the latch,
Sit by the fire and spin;
Take a cup
And drink it up,
And call your neighbours in.

Doctor Faustus was a good man,
He whipped his scholars now and then;
When he whipped them he made them dance
Out of England into France,
Out of France into Spain,
And then he whipped them back again!

Patience is a virtue,
Virtue is a grace;
Both put together
Make a very pretty face.

Great A, little a,
Bouncing B,
The cat's in the cupboard
And can't see me.

Pussy cat ate the dumplings, the dumplings,
Pussy cat ate the dumplings.
Mama stood by, and cried, "Oh, fie!
Why did you eat the dumplings?"

Hickle them, pickle them,
Catch them and tickle them;
I'll teach the villains to eat my fine pears!
Gobble them, hobble them,
Snatch them and bobble them,
Till all of them fancy they have fallen downstairs.

The Queen of Hearts,
She made some tarts,
All on a summer's day.
The Knave of Hearts,
He stole the tarts,
And took them clean away.

The King of Hearts
Called for the tarts,
And beat the Knave full sore.
The Knave of Hearts
Brought back the tarts,
And vowed he'd steal no more.

There was a little girl, who had a little curl
Right in the middle of her forehead;
When she was good she was very, very good,
But when she was bad, she was horrid.

Wine and cakes for gentlemen,
Hay and corn for horses,
A cup of ale for good old wives,
And kisses for young lasses.

A tisket, a tasket,
A green and yellow basket,
I wrote a letter to my love,
And on the way I dropped it.
    I dropped it,
    I dropped it,
And on the way I dropped it.
A little boy picked it up
And put it in his pocket.

The hart he loves the high wood,
The hare she loves the hill;
The knight he loves his bright sword,
The lady loves her will.

Yankee Doodle came to town,
Riding on a pony;
He stuck a feather in his cap
And called it macaroni.

Mrs Mason bought a basin.
Mrs Tyson said, "What a nice 'un!"
"What did it cost?" said Mrs Frost.
"Half a crown," said Mrs Brown.
"Did it, indeed?" said Mrs Reed.
"It did for certain," said Mrs Burton.
Then Mrs Nix, up to her tricks,
Threw the basin on the bricks.

My mill grinds pepper and spice;
Your mill grinds rats and mice.

142

There was an old woman sat spinning,
And that's the first beginning;
She had a calf,
And that's half;
She took it by the tail,
And threw it over the wall,
And that's all.

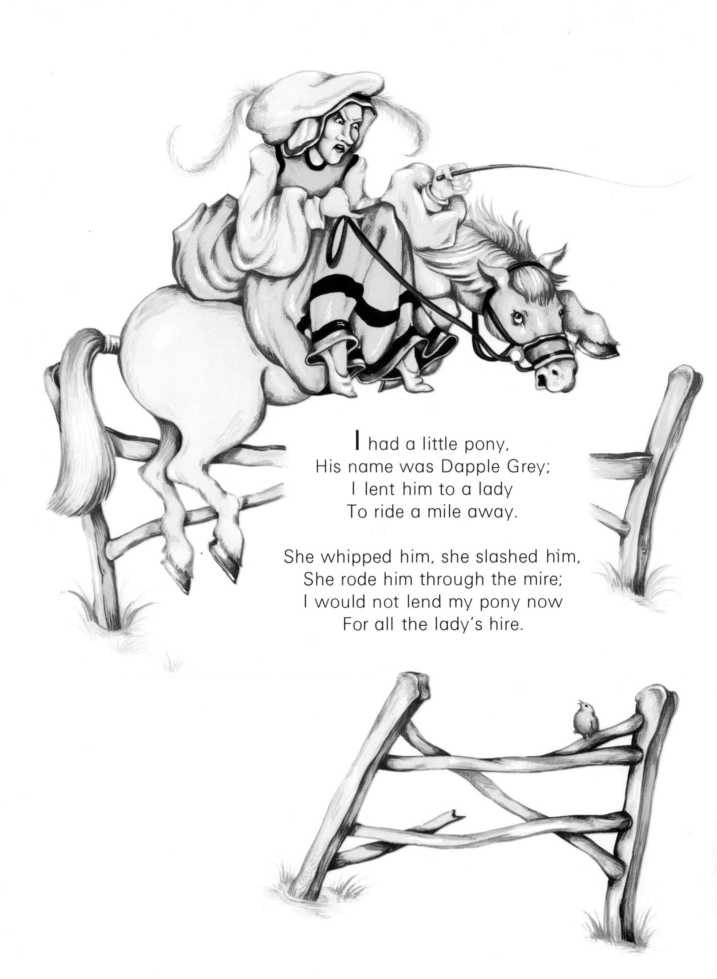

I had a little pony,
His name was Dapple Grey;
I lent him to a lady
To ride a mile away.

She whipped him, she slashed him,
She rode him through the mire;
I would not lend my pony now
For all the lady's hire.

As I was going up Pippin Hill,
Pippin Hill was dirty;
There I met a pretty Miss,
And she dropped me a curtsey.

Little Miss, pretty Miss,
Blessings light upon you;
If I had half a crown a day,
I'd spend it all upon you.

A man went a-hunting at Reigate,
And wished to leap over a high gate.
Says the owner, "Go round,
With your gun and your hound,
For you never shall jump over my gate."

I had a cat and the cat pleased me,
I fed my cat by yonder tree;
    Cat goes, "Fiddle-i-fee."

I had a hen and the hen pleased me,
I fed my hen by yonder tree;
    Hen goes, "Chimmy-chuck, chimmy-chuck,"
    Cat goes, "Fiddle-i-fee."

I had a duck and the duck pleased me,
I fed my duck by yonder tree;
    Duck goes, "Quack, quack,"
    Hen goes, "Chimmy-chuck, chimmy-chuck,"
    Cat goes, "Fiddle-i-fee."

I had a goose and the goose pleased me,
I fed my goose by yonder tree;
    Goose goes, "Swishy, swashy,"
    Duck goes, "Quack, quack,"
    Hen goes, "Chimmy-chuck, chimmy-chuck,"
    Cat goes, "Fiddle-i-fee."

I had a sheep and the sheep pleased me,
I fed my sheep by yonder tree;
    Sheep goes, "Baa, baa,"
    Goose goes, "Swishy, swashy,"
    Duck goes, "Quack, quack,"
    Hen goes, "Chimmy-chuck, chimmy-chuck,"
    Cat goes, "Fiddle-i-fee."

I had a pig and the pig pleased me,
I fed my pig by yonder tree;
    Pig goes, "Griffy, gruffy,"
    Sheep goes, "Baa, baa,"
    Goose goes, "Swishy, swashy,"
    Duck goes, "Quack, quack,"
    Hen goes, "Chimmy-chuck, chimmy-chuck,"
    Cat goes, "Fiddle-i-fee."

I had a cow and the cow pleased me,
I fed my cow by yonder tree;
    Cow goes, "Moo, moo,"
    Pig goes, "Griffy, gruffy,"
    Sheep goes, "Baa, baa,"
    Goose goes, "Swishy, swashy,"
    Duck goes, "Quack, quack,"
    Hen goes, "Chimmy-chuck, chimmy-chuck,"
    Cat goes, "Fiddle-i-fee."

I had a horse and the horse pleased me,
I fed my horse by yonder tree;
    Horse goes, "Neigh, neigh,"
    Cow goes, "Moo, moo,"
    Pig goes, "Griffy, gruffy,"
    Sheep goes, "Baa, baa,"
    Goose goes, "Swishy, swashy,"
    Duck goes, "Quack, quack,"
    Hen goes, "Chimmy-chuck, chimmy-chuck,"
    Cat goes, "Fiddle-i-fee."

I had a dog and the dog pleased me,
I fed my dog by yonder tree;
    Dog goes, "Bow-wow, bow-wow,"
    Horse goes, "Neigh, neigh,"
    Cow goes, "Moo, moo,"
    Pig goes, "Griffy, gruffy,"
    Sheep goes, "Baa, baa,"
    Goose goes, "Swishy, swashy,"
    Duck goes, "Quack, quack,"
    Hen goes, "Chimmy-chuck, chimmy-chuck,"
    Cat goes, "Fiddle-i-fee."

Jack be nimble;
Jack be quick;
Jack jump over
The candlestick.

Here we go round the mulberry bush,
The mulberry bush, the mulberry bush,
Here we go round the mulberry bush,
On a cold and frosty morning.

This is the way we wash our hands,
Wash our hands, wash our hands,
This is the way we wash our hands,
On a cold and frosty morning.

This is the way we wash our clothes,
Wash our clothes, wash our clothes,
This is the way we wash our clothes,
On a cold and frosty morning.

Sally go round the sun,
Sally go round the moon,
Sally go round the chimney-pots
On a Saturday afternoon.

This is the way we go to school,
Go to school, go to school,
This is the way we go to school,
On a cold and frosty morning.

This is the way we come out of school,
Come out of school, come out of school,
This is the way we come out of school,
On a cold and frosty morning.

149

Two little dickie-birds,
Sitting on a wall,
One named Peter,
The other named Paul;
Fly away, Peter! Fly away, Paul!
Come back, Peter! Come back, Paul!

In a cottage in Fife
Lived a man and his wife,
Who, believe me, were comical folk;
For, to people's surprise,
They both saw with their eyes,
And their tongues moved whenever they spoke.
When quite fast asleep,
I've been told that to keep
Their eyes open they could not contrive;
They walked on their feet,
And 'twas thought what they eat
Helped, with drinking, to keep them alive.

In the greenhouse lives a wren,
Little friend of little men;
When they're good she tells them where
To find the apple, quince and pear.

Mary, Mary, quite contrary,
How does your garden grow?
With silver bells and cockle shells,
And pretty maids all in a row.

The man in the wilderness asked of me,
"How many strawberries grow in the sea?"
I answered him, as I thought good,
"As many as herrings grow in the wood."

Robin Hood, Robin Hood,
Is in the mickle wood;
Little John, Little John,
He to the town is gone.

Robin Hood, Robin Hood,
Is telling his beads,
All in the greenwood,
Among the green weeds.

Little John, Little John,
If he comes no more,
Robin Hood, Robin Hood,
He will fret full sore!

NOTTINGHAM

II MILES

FRESH
PICKED
HERRINGS

There was an owl lived in an oak,
Wisky, wasky, weedle;
And every word he ever spoke
Was, "Fiddle, faddle, feedle."

A gunner chanced to come this way,
Wisky, wasky, weedle;
Says he, "I'll shoot you, silly bird."
Fiddle, faddle, feedle.

Ply the spade
And ply the hoe,
Plant the seed
And it will grow.

My mother said
That I never should
Play with the Gipsies
In the wood;
If I did she would say,
"Naughty girl to disobey.
Your hair shan't curl,
Your shoes shan't shine,
You naughty girl
You shan't be mine."
My father said
That if I did
He'd bang my head
With the teapot lid.

Cut thistles in May,
They grow in a day;
Cut them in June,
That is too soon;
Cut them in July,
Then they will die.

Sneeze on Monday, sneeze for danger;
Sneeze on Tuesday, kiss a stranger;
Sneeze on Wednesday, sneeze for a letter;
Sneeze on Thursday, something better;
Sneeze on Friday, sneeze for sorrow;
Sneeze on Saturday, joy for tomorrow.

Three little kittens,
They lost their mittens,
And they began to cry,
"Oh, mother dear,
we sadly fear
That we have lost our mittens."

"What! Lost your mittens,
You naughty kittens!
Then you shall have no pie.
Mee-ow, mee-ow, mee-ow.
No, you shall have no pie."

The three little kittens,
They found their mittens,
And they began to cry,
"Oh, mother dear, see here,
see here,
For we have found our mittens."

"What! Found your mittens,
You silly kittens!
Then you shall have some pie.
Purr-r, purr-r, purr-r,
Oh, let us have some pie."

Three little kittens,
Put on their mittens,
And soon ate up the pie;
"Oh, mother dear, we greatly fear
That we have soiled our mittens."

"What! Soiled your mittens,
You naughty kittens!"
Then they began to sigh,
"Mee-ow, mee-ow, mee-ow."
Then they began to sigh.

The three little kittens,
They washed their mittens,
And hung them out to dry;
"Oh, mother dear, do you not hear,
That we have washed our mittens?"

"What! Washed your mittens?
You're good little kittens.
But I smell a rat close by!
Hush! Hush! Hush!
I smell a rat close by."

There was a rat,
For want of stairs,
Went down a rope
To say his prayers.

The owl and the eel and the warming pan,
They went to call on the soap-fat man.
The soap-fat man, he was not within;
He'd gone for a ride on his rolling-pin;
So they all came back by the way of the town,
And turned the meeting house upside down.

There was an old crow
Sat upon a clod;
That's the end of my song.
That's odd.

Penny and penny
Laid up will be many;
Who will not save a penny
Shall never have many.

Barber, barber, shave a pig,
How many hairs to make a wig?
Four and twenty, that's enough.
Give the barber a pinch of snuff.

Dear, dear! What can the matter be?
Two old women got up in an apple tree;
One came down, and the other stayed
       till Saturday.

Elizabeth, Elspeth, Betsy and Bess,
They all went together to seek a bird's nest;
They found a bird's nest with five eggs in,
They all took one and left four in.

The dove says, "Coo, coo, what shall
      I do?
I can scarce maintain two."
"Pooh, pooh!" says the wren, "I've
      got ten,
And keep them all like gentlemen."

Little Robin Redbreast sat upon a rail;
Niddle-naddle went his head, wiggle-waggle went his tail.

Little Robin Redbreast sat upon a tree,
Up went Pussy Cat, and down went he.

Down came Pussy Cat, and away Robin ran;
Says little Robin Redbreast, "Catch me if you can."

Little Robin Redbreast jumped upon a wall;
Pussy Cat jumped after him, and almost got a fall.

Little Robin chirped and sang, and what did Pussy say?
Pussy Cat said, "Mew," and Robin jumped away.

Ding, dong, bell,
Pussy's in the well.
Who put her in?
Little Johnny Green.
Who pulled her out?
Little Tommy Stout.
What a naughty boy was that
To try to drown poor pussy cat,
Which never did him any harm,
But killed the mice in his father's barn.

There was a maid on Scrabble Hill,
And if not dead, she lives there still;
She grew so tall, she reached the sky,
And on the moon, hung clothes to dry.

Jack and Jill went up the hill
To fetch a pail of water;
Jack fell down and broke his crown,
And Jill came tumbling after.

Then up Jack got and home did trot,
As fast as he could caper.
They put him to bed and plastered his head
With vinegar and brown paper.

Blow, wind, blow! and go, mill, go!
That the miller may grind his corn;
That the baker may take it,
And into bread make it,
And bring us a loaf in the morn.

Monday alone,
Tuesday together,
Wednesday we walk
When it's fine weather,
Thursday we kiss,
Friday we cry,
Saturday's hours
Seem almost to fly.
But of all the days
Of the week we will call
Sunday, the rest day,
The best day of all.

All work and no play,
Makes Jack a dull boy;
All play and no work,
Makes Jack a mere toy.

There was a little man, and he had a little gun,
And his bullets were made of lead, lead, lead;
He went to the brook, and shot a little duck,
Right through the middle of the head, head, head.

He carried it home to his old wife Joan,
And bade her a fire to make, make, make;
To roast the little duck he had shot in the brook,
And he'd go and fetch her the drake, drake, drake.

The little drake was swimming, with his little curly tail,
And the little man made his mark, mark, mark;
He let off his gun, but he fired too soon,
And away flew the drake with a quack, quack, quack.

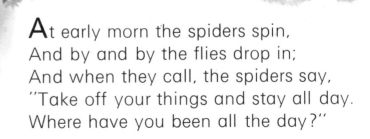

At early morn the spiders spin,
And by and by the flies drop in;
And when they call, the spiders say,
"Take off your things and stay all day.
Where have you been all the day?"

A million little diamonds
Twinkled on the trees;
And all the little maidens said,
"A jewel, if you please!"
But while they held their hands outstretched,
To catch the diamonds gay,
A million little sunbeams came,
And stole them all away.

Lavender's blue, dilly dilly,
  Lavender's green;
When I am king, dilly dilly,
  You shall be queen.

Who told you so, dilly dilly,
  Who told you so?
'Twas mine own heart, dilly dilly,
  That told me so.

When I was a little girl,
About seven years old,
I hadn't got a petticoat
To keep me from the cold.

So I went into Darlington,
That pretty little town,
And there I bought a petticoat,
A cloak and a gown.

Where are you going to, my pretty maid?
"I'm going a-milking, sir," she said.

May I go with you, my pretty maid?
"You're kindly welcome, sir," she said.

Say, will you marry me, my pretty maid?
"Yes, if you please, kind sir," she said.

What is your fortune, my pretty maid?
"My face is my fortune, sir," she said.

Then I can't marry you, my pretty maid.
"Nobody asked you, sir," she said.

There was a man of Thessaly
And he was wondrous wise,
He jumped into a bramble bush
And scratched out both his eyes.
And when he saw his eyes were out,
With all his might and main
He jumped into another bush
And scratched them in again.

Little Tommy Tittlemouse
Lived in a little house;
He caught fishes
In other men's ditches.

Leg over leg,
As the dog went to Dover;
When he came to a stile,
Jump, he went over.

Charlie Warlie had a cow,
Black and white about the brow;
Open the gate and let her through,
Charley Warlie's old cow.

A little pig found a fifty-pound note
And purchased a hat and a very fine coat,
With trousers and stockings and shoes,
Cravat and shirt-collar and gold-headed cane;
Then proud as could be, did he march up the lane,
Says he, "I shall hear all the news."

Gilly Silly Jarter,
She lost her garter,
In a shower of rain.
The miller found it,
The miller ground it,
And the miller gave it to Silly again.

There was a little boy went into a barn
And lay down on some hay;
An owl came out and flew about,
And the little boy ran away.

173

Three young rats with black felt hats,
Three young ducks with new straw flats,
Three young dogs with curling tails,
Three young cats with demi-veils,
Went out to walk with two young pigs,
In satin vests and sorrel wigs;
But suddenly it chanced to rain,
And so they all went home again.

Bessy Bell and Mary Gray,
They were two bonnie lasses;
They built their house upon the lea,
And covered it with rushes.

Bessy kept the garden gate,
And Mary kept the pantry;
Bessy always had to wait,
While Mary lived in plenty.

Two little dogs
Sat by the fire,
Over a fender of coal-dust;
Said one little dog
To the other little dog,
"If you don't talk, why, I must."

There were three crooks of Colebrook,
And they fell out with our cook;
And all was for a pudding he took
From the three cooks of Colebrook.

Anna Elise, she jumped with surprise;
The surprise was so quick, it played her a trick;
The trick was so rare, she jumped in a chair;
The chair was so frail, she jumped in a pail;
The pail was so wet, she jumped in a net;
The net was so small, she jumped on the ball;
The ball was so round, she jumped on the ground;
And ever since then she's been turning around.

Grandfa' Grig
Had a pig,
In a field of clover;
Piggie died,
Grandfa' cried,
And all the fun was over.

The barber shaved the mason,
As I suppose,
Cut off his nose,
And popped it in a basin.

177

A cat came fiddling out of a barn,
With a pair of bagpipes under her arm;
She could sing nothing but fiddle-de-dee,
The mouse has married the bumble bee;
Pipe, cat; dance mouse,
We'll have a wedding at our good house.

The daughter of the farrier
Could find no one to marry her,
    Because she said
    She would not wed
A man who could not carry her.

The foolish girl was wrong enough,
And had to wait quite long enough;
    For as she sat
    She grew so fat
That nobody was strong enough!

Oh, Mother, I shall be married
To Mr Punchinello,
To Mr Punch,
To Mr Joe;
To Mr Nell,
To Mr Low,
To Mr Punch, Mr Joe,
Mr Nell, Mr Low,
Mr Punchinello.

On Saturday night
Shall be my care
To powder my locks
And curl my hair.

On Sunday morning
My love will come in,
When he will marry me
With a gold ring.

179

The farmer in the dell,
The farmer in the dell,
Heigho! the derry oh,
The farmer in the dell.

The farmer takes a wife,
The farmer takes a wife,
Heigho! the derry oh,
The farmer takes a wife.

The wife takes the child,
The wife takes the child,
Heigho! the derry oh,
The wife takes the child.

The child takes the nurse,
The child takes the nurse,
Heigho! the derry oh,
The child takes the nurse.

The nurse takes the dog,
The nurse takes the dog
Heigho! the derry oh,
The nurse takes the dog

The dog takes the cat,
The dog takes the cat,
Heigho! the derry oh,
The dog takes the cat.

The cat takes the rat,
The cat takes the rat,
Heigho! the derry oh,
The cat takes the rat.

The rat takes the cheese,
The rat takes the cheese,
Heigho! the derry oh,
The rat takes the cheese.

The cheese stands alone,
The cheese stands alone,
Heigho! the derry oh,
The cheese stands alone.

We're all in the dumps,
For diamonds are trumps,
The kittens are gone to St Paul's!
The babies are bit,
The moon's in a fit,
And the houses are built without walls.

My father died a month ago
And left me all his riches;
A feather bed, a wooden leg,
And a pair of leather breeches;
A coffee pot without a spout,
A cup without a handle,
A tobacco pipe without a lid,
And half a farthing candle.

Little Nanny Etticoat
In a white petticoat
And a red nose;
The longer she stands
The shorter she grows.

Old Toby Sizer is such a miser,
No cloak he'll buy to keep him dry, sir.
He'll not permit his neighbour, Randal,
To light his pipe by his short candle,
For fear, he says, he might convey
A little bit of light away.

Peter White will never go right.
Do you know the reason why?
He follows his nose wherever he goes,
And that stands all awry.

Ladybird! Ladybird! fly away home;
Your house is on fire, your children all gone;
All but one, and her name is Ann,
And she crept under the pudding pan.

Old Mother Shuttle
Lived in a coal scuttle,
Along with her dog and her cat;
What they ate I can't tell,
But it's known very well
That none of the party was fat.

There was a crooked man, and he went a crooked mile,
He found a crooked sixpence against a crooked stile;
He bought a crooked cat, which caught a crooked mouse,
And they all lived together in a little crooked house.

What are you doing, my lady, my lady,
What are you doing, my lady?

    I'm spinning old breeches, good body, good body,
    I'm spinning old breeches, good body.

      Long may you wear them, my lady, my lady,
      Long may you wear them, my lady.

      I'll wear 'em and tear 'em, good body, good body,
      I'll wear 'em and tear 'em, good body.

    I was sweeping my room, my lady, my lady,
    I was sweeping my room, my lady.

      I found me a sixpence, my lady, my lady,
      I found me a sixpence, my lady.

    The richer you were, good body, good body,
    The richer you were, good body.

  I went to the market, my lady, my lady,
  I went to the market, my lady.

    The further you went, good body, good body,
    The further you went, good body.

    I bought me a pudding, my lady, my lady,
    I bought me a pudding, my lady.

The more meat you had, good body, good body,
The more meat you had, good body.

I put it in the window to cool, my lady,
I put it in the window to cool.

The faster you'd eat it, good body, good body,
The faster you'd eat it, good body.

The cat came and ate it, my lady, my lady,
The cat came and ate it, my lady.

And I'll eat you too, good body, good body,
And I'll eat you too, good body.

If I had a donkey that wouldn't go,
Would I beat him? Oh no, no.
I'd put him in the barn and give him some corn,
The best little donkey that ever was born.

Is John Smith within?
Yes, that he is.
Can he set a shoe?
Ay, marry, two.
Here a nail, there a nail,
Tick, tack, too.

NAILS NAILS

Dickory, dickory, dare,
The pig flew up in the air;
The man in brown soon brought him down,
Dickory, dickory, dare.

Peter, Peter, pumpkin-eater,
Had a wife and couldn't keep her;
He put her in a pumpkin shell,
And there he kept her very well.

Nose, nose, jolly red nose,
And what gave you that jolly red nose?
Nutmegs and ginger, spices and cloves,
That's what gave me this jolly red nose.

I'll tell you a story
About Jack a Nory,
And now my story's begun;
I'll tell you another
Of Jack and his brother,
And now my story is done.

Fee, fi, foe, fum,
I smell the blood of an Englishman;
Be he alive or be he dead,
I'll grind his bones to make my bread.

Robin the Bobbin,
     the big-bellied Ben,
He ate more meat
     than fourscore men;
He ate a cow,
     he ate a calf,
He ate a butcher
     and a half,
He ate a church,
     he ate a steeple,
He ate a priest
     and all the people!
A cow and a calf,
An ox and a half,
A church and a steeple
And all the good people,
And yet he complained
     that his stomach wasn't full.

191

As I was going to sell my eggs,
I met a man with bandy legs,
Bandy legs and crooked toes,
I tripped up his heels
and he fell on his nose.

Little maiden, better tarry;
Time enough next year to marry.
Hearts may change,
And so may fancy;
Wait a little longer, Nancy.

192

What are little boys made of, made of?
What are little boys made of?
Frogs and snails, and puppy-dogs' tails,
That's what little boys are made of.

What are little girls made of, made of?
What are little girls made of?
Sugar and spice, and all things nice;
That's what little girls are made of.

Cow, cow, come blow your horn,
And you shall have a peck of corn.

Little Boy Blue,
Come blow your horn!
The sheep's in the meadow,
The cow's in the corn.

But where is the boy
Who looks after the sheep?
He's under a haycock
Fast asleep!

Will you wake him?
No, not I;
For if I do,
He's sure to cry.

As I was going up the hill,
I met with Jack the piper;
And all the tune that he could play
Was, "Tie up your petticoats tighter".

I tied them once, I tied them twice,
I tied them three times over;
And all the song that he could sing
Was, "Carry me safe to Dover".

195

This old man, he played one,
He played knick-knack on my drum,
Knick-knack, paddy whack,
Give a dog a bone,
This old man came rolling home.

This old man, he played two,
He played knick-knack on my shoe,
Knick-knack, paddy whack,
Give a dog a bone,
This old man came rolling home.

This old man, he played three
He played knick-knack on my knee,
Knick-knack, paddy whack,
Give a dog a bone,
This old man came rolling home.

Cock-a-doodle-doo!
My dame has lost her shoe,
My master's lost his fiddling stick,
And knows not what to do.

Cock-a-doodle-doo!
What is my dame to do?
Till master finds his fiddling stick
She'll dance without her shoe.

Cock-a-doodle-doo!
My dame has found her shoe,
And master's found his fiddling stick,
Sing doodle doodle doo.

Cock-a-doodle-doo!
My dame will dance with you,
While master fiddles his fiddling stick
For dame and doodle-doo.

I'll sing you a song,
Nine verses long,
    For a pin;
Three and three are six,
And three are nine;
You are a fool,
    And the pin is mine.

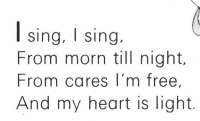

I sing, I sing,
From morn till night,
From cares I'm free,
And my heart is light.

Tom, he was a piper's son,
He learned to play when he was young,
But all the tune that he could play
Was, "Over the hills and far away"
Over the hills and a great way off,
The wind shall blow my top-knot off.

Tom with his pipe did play with
        such skill
That those who heard him could
        never keep still;
As soon as he played they began
        for to dance,
Even pigs on their hind legs would
        after him prance.
Over the hills and a great way off,
The wind shall blow my top-knot off.

Go to bed late,
Stay very small;
Go to bed early,
Grow very tall.

Wee Willie Winkie runs through the town,
Upstairs and downstairs, in his nightgown;
Rapping at the window, crying through the lock,
"Are the children all in bed, for now it's eight o'clock?"

Friday night's dream
On Saturday told,
Is sure to come true,
Be it never so old.

"To bed, to bed!" says Sleepy-head.
"Tarry awhile," says Slow.
"Put on the pan," says greedy Nan.
"We'll sup before we go."

Diddle, diddle, dumpling, my son John,
Went to bed with his trousers on;
One shoe off, and one shoe on;
Diddle, diddle, dumpling, my son John.

I went up one pair of stairs.
    Just like me.
I went up two pairs of stairs.
    Just like me.
I went into a room.
    Just like me.
I looked out of a window.
    Just like me.
And there I saw a monkey.
    Just like me!

Good night,
Sleep tight.

Wake up bright,
In the morning light,
To do what's right
With all your might.

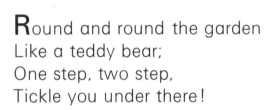

Round and round the garden
Like a teddy bear;
One step, two step,
Tickle you under there!

"To make your candles last for aye,
You wives and maids give ear-O!
To put them out's the only way,"
Says honest John Boldero.

Hush, little baby, don't say a word,
Papa's going to buy you a mocking bird.

If the mocking bird won't sing,
Papa's going to buy you a diamond ring.

If the diamond ring turns to brass,
Papa's going to buy you a looking-glass.

If the looking-glass gets broke,
Papa's going to buy you a billy-goat.

If that billy-goat runs away,
Papa's going to buy you another today.

202

Ride a cock-horse to Banbury Cross,
To see a fine lady upon a white horse;
Rings on her fingers and bells on her toes,
She shall have music wherever she goes.

Rock-a-bye, baby, on the tree top,
When the wind blows the cradle will rock;
When the bough breaks the cradle will fall,
Down will come baby, cradle and all.

Moses supposes his toeses are roses,
But Moses supposes erroneously;
For nobody's toeses are posies of roses
As Moses supposes his toeses to be.

There was an old woman who lived in a shoe.
She had so many children she didn't know
what to do.
She gave them some broth without any bread,
And whipped them all soundly and put
them to bed.

Up the wooden hill to Bedfordshire,
Down Sheet Lane to Blanket Fair.

I see the moon,
And the moon sees me;
God bless the moon,
And God bless me.

Matthew, Mark, Luke, and John,
Bless the bed that I lie on.
All four corners round about,
When I get in, when I get out.

Four corners to my bed,
Four angels round my head;
One to watch and one to pray,
And two to bear my soul away.

There was a man lived in the moon, lived in the moon,
      lived in the moon,
There was a man lived in the moon,
And his name was Aiken Drum.
And he played upon a ladle, a ladle, a ladle,
And he played upon a ladle,
And his name was Aiken Drum.

And his hat was made of good cream cheese,
      good cream cheese, good cream cheese,
And his hat was made of good cream cheese,
And his name was Aiken Drum.

And his coat was made of good roast beef,
      good roast beef, good roast beef,
And his coat was made of good roast beef,
And his name was Aiken Drum.

What is the news of the day,
Good neighbour, I pray?
They say the balloon
Is gone up to the moon!

And his buttons were made of penny loaves,
penny loaves, penny loaves,
And his buttons were made of penny loaves,
And his name was Aiken Drum.

His waistcoat was made of crust of pies,
crust of pies, crust of pies,
His waistcoat was made of crust of pies,
And his name was Aiken Drum.

His breeches were made of haggis bags,
haggis bags, haggis bags,
His breeches were made of haggis bags,
And his name was Aiken Drum.

Hey diddle, diddle,
The cat and the fiddle,
The cow jumped over the moon;
The little dog laughed
To see such sport,
And the dish ran away with the spoon.

Bye, baby bunting,
Daddy's gone a-hunting,
To get a little rabbit's skin
To wrap his baby bunting in.

Pease porridge hot,
Pease porridge cold,
Pease porridge in the pot,
Nine days old.

Some like it hot,
Some like it cold,
Some like it in the pot,
Nine days old.

Old woman, old woman, shall we go a-shearing?
Speak a little louder, sir, I'm very hard of hearing.
Old woman, old woman, shall I kiss you dearly?
Thank you very kindly, sir, I hear you very clearly.

There was a monkey climbed a tree,
When he fell down, then down fell he.

Sing, sing, what shall I sing?
The cat's run away with the pudding-string!
Do, do, what shall I do?
The cat has bitten it quite in two.

The first day of Christmas,
My true love sent to me
        A partridge in a pear tree.

The second day of Christmas,
My true love sent to me
        Two turtle doves and
        A partridge in a pear tree.

The third day of Christmas,
My true love sent to me
        Three French hens,
        Two turtle doves and
        A partridge in a pear tree.

The fourth day of Christmas,
My true love sent to me
        Four colly birds,
        Three French hens,
        Two turtle doves and
        A partridge in a pear tree.

The fifth day of Christmas,
My true love sent to me
    Five gold rings,
    Four colly birds,
    Three French hens,
    Two turtle doves and
    A partridge in a pear tree.

The sixth day of Christmas,
My true love sent to me
    Six geese a-laying,
    Five gold rings,
    Four colly birds,
    Three French hens,
    Two turtle doves and
    A partridge in a pear tree.

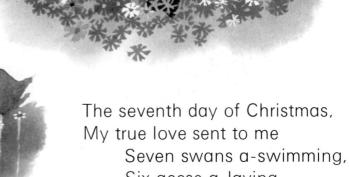

The seventh day of Christmas,
My true love sent to me
    Seven swans a-swimming,
    Six geese a-laying,
    Five gold rings,
    Four colly birds,
    Three French hens,
    Two turtle doves and
    A partridge in a pear tree.

The eighth day of Christmas,
My true love sent to me
    Eight maids a-milking,
    Seven swans a-swimming,
    Six geese a-laying,
    Five gold rings,
    Four colly birds,
    Three French hens,
    Two turtle doves and
    A partridge in a pear tree.

The ninth day of Christmas,
My true love sent to me
    Nine drummers drumming,
    Eight maids a-milking,
    Seven swans a-swimming,
    Six geese a-laying,
    Five gold rings,
    Four colly birds,
    Three French hens,
    Two turtle doves and
    A partridge in a pear tree.

The tenth day of Christmas,
My true love sent to me
    Ten pipers piping,
    Nine drummers drumming,
    Eight maids a-milking,
    Seven swans a-swimming,
    Six geese a-laying,
    Five gold rings,
    Four colly birds,
    Three French hens,
    Two turtle doves and
    A partridge in a pear tree.

The eleventh day of Christmas,
My true love sent to me
　　Eleven ladies dancing,
　　Ten pipers piping,
　　Nine drummers drumming,
　　Eight maids a-milking,
　　Seven swans a-swimming,
　　Six geese a-laying,
　　Five gold rings,
　　Four colly birds,
　　Three French hens,
　　Two turtle doves and
　　A partridge in a pear tree.

The twelfth day of Christmas,
My true love sent to me
　　Twelve lords a-leaping,
　　Eleven ladies dancing,
　　Ten pipers piping,
　　Nine drummers drumming,
　　Eight maids a-milking,
　　Seven swans a-swimming,
　　Six geese a-laying,
　　Five gold rings,
　　Four colly birds,
　　Three French hens,
　　Two turtle doves and
　　A partridge in a pear tree.

Jingle, bells! Jingle, bells!
Jingle all the way;
Oh, what fun it is to ride
In a one-horse open sleigh.

Christmas is coming, the geese are getting fat;
Please to put a penny in the old man's hat;
If you haven't got a penny, a ha'penny will do.
If you haven't got a ha'penny, God bless you.

Snow, snow faster,
Ally-ally-blaster;
The old woman's plucking her geese,
Selling the feathers a penny a piece.

On Christmas Eve I turned the spit;
I burnt my fingers, I feel it yet;
The cock sparrow flew over the table,
The pot began to play with the ladle;
The ladle stood up like an angry man,
And vowed he'd fight the frying pan;
The frying pan behind the door
Said he never saw the like before;
And the kitchen clock I was going to wind,
Said he never saw the like behind.

Dame, get up and bake your pies,
Bake your pies, bake your pies,
Dame, get up and bake your pies
On Christmas Day in the morning.

Little Jack Horner sat in the corner,
Eating a Christmas pie;
He put in his thumb, and he pulled out a plum,
And said, "What a good boy am I!"

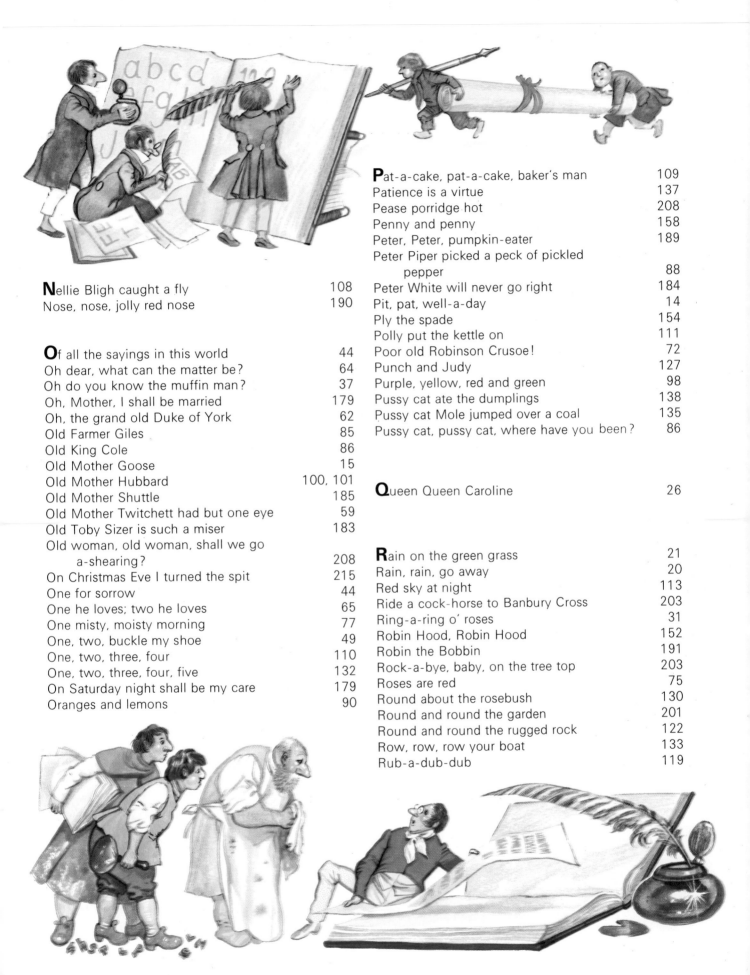

221